CRANNÓG 47 autumn 2018

Editorial Board

Sandra Bunting
Ger Burke
Jarlath Fahy
Tony O'Dwyer

ISSN 1649-4865
ISBN 978-1-907017-50-6

Cover image: Flight 126 (Stars) by Ruth McHugh
Cover image sourced by Sandra Bunting
Cover design by Wordsonthestreet
Published by Wordsonthestreet for Crannóg magazine
www.wordsonthestreet.com @wordsstreet

All writing copyrighted to rightful owners in accordance with The Berne Convention

CONTENTS

Thirty-five a Night
   Shauna Gilligan 7
The Spanish Steps, Rome
   Byron Beynon 10
Ancestral Song
   Maureen Weldon 11
Yield
   Aoife Reilly 12
Worrywart
   Brian Kirk 13
The Weight of a Song in My Mouth
   James C. Bassett 14
I Never Tire of the Moon
   Stephanie Roberts 17
There She Goes Again
   Sasha Burshteyn 18
As If
   Gill McEvoy 19
Grey Sky, Raindrops on the Window
   Richard W. Halperin 20
The Workhouse
   Claire Loader 21
Mothering Sunday and a Blackbird Has Ice-Cream on Its Beak
   Alice West 24
Combing the Hair ('La Coiffure')
   Ciarán O'Rourke 26
Sounding 36
   Ray Malone 27
Beth
   Susan Millar DuMars 28
Dear future occupants,
   Laurinda Lind 33
Ungeheures Ungeziefer
   Anne Walsh Donnelly 34
Death Of Cuchulainn?
   Michael Casey 35
Morning Room
   Maria Isakova Bennett 36
The Tea Ceremony
   Clare McCotter 37
Cleaning the Labyrinth
   Lauren Camp 41
Love Me Anyway
   Kory Wells 42

Where Are We Going
  Karla Van Vliet..44
Atlantic Leather Co.
  Douglas W. Milliken 45
Even a Monkey
  Lisa C. Taylor..46
Rising
  Vinny Steed 49
Sisyphus in Paradise
  Michael Derrick Hudson..50
Golden Boughs
  Mary O'Brien 52
Coming of Age
  Ellen Denton 53
Unleaving
  Ruth Thompson 57
Stalled Childhood
  Okwudili Nebeolisa 58
Finding Madrid
  Eamon Mc Guinness..60
Amateur Escapologists
  John Wall Barger 61
Animal
  Alison McCrossan 62
My View of Things
  Kevin Higgins..64
The Meaning of the Dog Digging in the Grass
  Laura Foley...66
Losing Sight
  Jean Tuomey..67
And I Will Come Running
  Joe Davies...68
reset: in the kitchen sometime after midnight but well before dawn
  Barbara Turney Wieland..72
Winter Wasp
  Laura McKee 73
The Tribes of Grass
  Nancy Holmes 74
The Secret Names of Objects
  Jonathan Greenhause 75
The Crannóg Questionnaire
  Alan McMonagle..76
Artist's Statement
  Ruth McHugh 80
Biographical Details 81

The Galway Study Centre

Since 1983, the Galway Study Centre has been dedicating itself to giving an excellent education service to post-primary school students in Galway.

info@galwaystudycentre.ie
Tel: 091-564254

www.galwaystudycentre.ie

BRIDGE MILLS
GALWAY LANGUAGE CENTRE
Established 1987

Small family run language school
ACELS and MEI RELSA approved
Courses in English, Italian, Polish, Portuguese, Spanish, German and Japanese
Teacher training including CELT TEFL

Telephone: +353 (0) 91 566 468 Fax: +353 (0) 91 564 122
Email: info@galwaylanguage.com

Submissions for Crannóg 48 open March 1st until March 31st
Publication date is June 29th 2018

Crannóg is published three times a year in spring, summer and autumn.

Submission Times: Month of November for spring issue. Month of March for summer issue. Month of July for autumn issue.

We will not read submissions sent outside these times.

POETRY: Send no more than three poems. Each poem should be under 50 lines.

PROSE: Send one story. Stories should be under 2,000 words.

We do not accept postal submissions.

When emailing your submission we require **three** *things:*

1. *The text of your submission included both in body of email and as a Word attachment (this is to ensure correct layout. We may, however, change your layout to suit our publication).*
2. *A brief bio in the third person. Include this both in body and in attachment.*
3. *A postal address for contributor's copy in the event of publication.*

To learn more about Crannóg magazine, purchase copies of the current issue, or take out a subscription, log on to our website:

www.crannogmagazine.com

facebook
You Tube
twitter

THIRTY-FIVE A NIGHT   SHAUNA GILLIGAN

We have our routine, John and I. Every Saturday night we follow winding roads to an old hotel or a long-standing bed-and-breakfast in the countryside where we watch, in streak-free mirrors, the scenes we create on king-sized beds. In Dingle I am Madonna; in Cork I become Marianne Faithfull; in Galway I have the allure of Eva Braun. John dons one of his moustaches and heeled boots; a signet ring and a medallion; a tasselled studded jacket. For those few hours we are anywhere and anyone but civil servants who live in old houses with aging parents.

But this weekend we're not in the country; for €35 a night we can stay in Dublin and experiment, that's what John's decided. And so we cruise through the Phoenix Park in John's shiny Volvo, see a couple jogging in matching tracksuits, pass pretty white benches. There are people curled up on them, already sleeping. I think of what Maeve, my work pal, said to me earlier: if I could describe John in one word, then I'd know. I sorted through heaps of payroll claims before I landed on a word. *Considerate*. Maeve chewed on the lid of her pen.

'You mean in that he considers what you like, that sort of thing?'

'Yeah.'

'Sounds like the marrying type.'

More than being a wife, I want to feel what it is to be the woman for whom a man would give up his life. We cruise out through the ornate gates of the Park and a flutter of excitement runs through me. I feel the throb and pinch of new patent heels on my feet, think of the new lacy pants from Marks in my bag.

'So,' John says as he finishes parallel parking opposite the bed-and-breakfast. He turns off the engine, looks at me. He never likes to look directly at people, so when he gazes at me with a strange brightness in his eyes I feel I'm falling. Or maybe I've already fallen.

I look away; take in the neon light – *Thirty-Five-A-Night* – hanging from the red-brick Victorian with its garden of dying pink roses. I'm suddenly afraid. Maeve told me that in circumstances beyond our control we all have a choice: to laugh or to cry. I laugh.

'Well, Margo, they say a change is as good as a rest,' John says breezily getting out of the car, going to the boot for the bags.

He holds my door open then I follow him across the road, dodging traffic. So this is the first part of his experiment, I think. Not using pedestrian lights. John pushes open the navy-blue door with the polished brasses. I stand on the threshold trying to figure out the smell; some sort of lavender incense, or maybe one of those artificial sprays. The receptionist chews on pink gum as she stares at the computer screen. Click-click goes the mouse. She stops, and looks at us with a grin.

'Here we are so. I believe congratulations are in order.'

John shakes his head.

She cackles. 'Oh. Sorry about that. I'm getting you confused with *two-five-three*. Oops!'

She looks at me, a sort of pitiful look and I flick my newly straightened plum hair over my shoulder.

'Room 353, top of the stairs, you're alright without a lift?'

She hands John the key with a wink and I feel myself bristle.

'Let's go,' he says, turning to me, a little pink in the face.

I climb the steep stairs slowly, picturing myself stumbling in the patent black heels and breaking my ankle. And instead of our night of experiments – my throat goes dry again at the thought – we'll have a night in A&E.

But we reach the top of the stairs, finally, and John puts the bags on the floor with a sigh. He fumbles with the door lock and key. Shooting pains run from my legs to my back. I sigh and step out of the shoes, wiggle my toes on the old carpet.

'Got it.' John's delighted with himself.

I pick up the shoes and follow him into the room, my eyes adjusting to the darkness. There's a smell of sex and the beat of silence feels heavy until the lights come on.

'Well?' John turns to me, smiling.

The room – carpet, walls, lampshades, curtains, and bedspread – is completely 1980s, alarmingly like my teenage bedroom, minus the Duran Duran posters.

I stare at him. 'Peach, the whole room is peach.'

'The same as your Debs dress. The dress you wore when you danced with Paul Jones instead of me.'

I remember John at the Debs, standing in a corner with a scowl on his face, but I can't recall poor Paul Jones properly. I notice the grubby fringe on the bedspread that hangs to the floor. 'Horrible colour now that I look at it.'

I follow John's gaze to a peach dress hanging on the back of the door.

'It's your wedding dress, Margo,' he whispers fiercely.

I go to ask if he wants me to wear it tonight – a bride in Dublin! – but he's down on one knee and staring right at me.

The patent heels slide from my hand onto the floor with a thud. Now I *know*; I *do*. With my palms sweating and my heart pounding I feel the round of the *o* in the loud *NO* as it races up from my throat and tumbles right out of my mouth.

THE SPANISH STEPS, ROME — BYRON BEYNON

i.m. John Keats, 1795 - 1821

The afternoon ends,
an open bedroom window
looks down at razor-dressed Italians,
guide book tourists,
a stall ablaze with flowers.
The boat-shaped fountain by Pietro Bernini,
aground near the Spanish Steps
is broken and boarded.
The calm insides of No. 26
Piazza di Spagna retain
books of poetry, portraits,
life and death masks,
a letter from a President,
the brief note signed by Thomas Hardy,
each the formal remains of another age
on display.
The fireplace is like ice
in these repaired rooms
where the furniture was taken and burnt,
the walls scraped.
I stand in a small space
where death entered at eleven o'clock,
then leave by the staircase
he painfully climbed.
A life lived for poetry echoes and says
'that which is creative must create itself.'

ANCESTRAL SONG   MAUREEN WELDON

I might have remained in the sea,
whale, dolphin
or just a bubble trying to break free.

The two thousand year old tree,
drinking rain, drinking sun.
And look:

a rainbow – that long ago
sign from God.

I clamp my hand over my mouth,
that I, like the condor bird
or the arctic bear, tonight

through a hundred million bright stars,
listen to the primeval voice singing.

YIELD

AOIFE REILLY

You are stripping the last of the berries
from the elder's purple branches.
I am watching hawthorn release
a crimson transfusion across the land
to hold us in the death of light.
the leaves surrender despite us,
whitebeam, guelder, rose, elder,
Mercury, Venus, Earth, Mars.
These earth to sky maps we carry
from hedgerow to table
with blackened hands in bowls of foraged faith,
me and you trying to gather
what serves in the dark,
our lives, a scattered asteroid
between these fires
we will light in the night woods
to catch the chat
between wind and leaf
talking us through our creaks on the wheel,
my struggle, your resistance,
and these berries
from bud to bloom reaching into
the life behind the life,
the yield of what was sown,
berries that answered
a flower's prayer for fulfilment.

WORRYWART

BRIAN KIRK

With every step I feel the blister's bite
and so I stop, take off my shoes, and rest.
I know it's there, I touch it, I'm obsessed
by it. At dinner I can smile despite
the pain, but will not talk about my plight.
It needles me like an unwanted guest
who won't go home and I feel dispossessed.
The day is bad but nothing like the night;
I lie awake, your arm across my chest.
I watched in silence while you got undressed
last night – the ache. I try to put my best
foot forward, wonder do you feel contrite.
The self-inflicted hurt becomes intense.
I tell myself: *she loves you, please see sense.*

THE WEIGHT OF A SONG IN MY MOUTH
JAMES C. BASSETT

This frozen song weighs heavy in my mouth. A song should be light and liquid, but this song presses down on my tongue, aching my jaw. Its rough surface abrades my teeth and flays my tongue, but it is too big and solid for me to spit out.

Pythagoras – he of the theorem and the ban on beans – said a stone is frozen music. Music is a living thing, a flowing thing of pattern and pulse. Every atom vibrates at its own frequency, so we know now that Pythagoras was right, that stones are the pulsing patterns of music in calcified form. Calcify, from the Ancient Greek χάλιξ, kháliks, meaning pebble. Pythagoras would have used pebbles in an abacus for counting and calculating. Calculate, from the Latin calculus, a stone used for counting. Stones and mathematics and music have always been associated.

A stone can be a tool for counting; broken, chipped, a stone can become a weapon or it can become a work of art; a stone can be a thing of pain or a thing of beauty. A common joke about sculpting is that it is easy – all you do is chip away everything that isn't the sculpture that waits within the raw stone.

But anyone who has ever carved stone knows this is a facile joke, a casual untruth to misdirect the ignorant and the unknowing. Carving a stone is not merely liberating a thing that lies fully formed and already separate within the block, like a dinosaur bone, its hardness and colour making it obvious and easy to pick out. The sculpture within cannot be seen at all for what it is, but only felt.

And here is the true secret: carving is a negative process. One does not carve something out of stone, but into space. One does not chip away the excess stone; rather, one leaves behind the stone that fills the excess space.

A stone from space, an asteroid, crashed into the earth 66 million years ago, smashing into the planet with such force that the impact made the earth's surface move like a liquid, unfrozen, even though it remained solid rock. The effects of this cataclysm killed off the dinosaurs, and their bodies sank into the ground where other life, scavengers and microbes, consumed their flesh, leaving only the bones for time to eat, to calcify, to petrify, to freeze into rock.

An asteroid is not a chip carved off of a planet, but a stone that never coalesced into a planet to begin with. Millions of asteroids circle the sun in a narrow orbit between Mars and Jupiter, where gravity would have crushed them together into a planet if the gravity of the other planets had not spread them out and prevented their coming together as one.

The orbits of the planets (and the asteroids) exhibit a harmonic pattern. Their distances from the sun are determined by the same mathematical relationship that governs musical notes. Each planet occupies its own orbit, distinct as notes on a scale. The music of the spheres is a living performance of frozen music. This music creates harmony in the heavens, but this harmony can only exist through isolation. The planets interact only distantly through gravity, never to risk a closer touch, a collision.

Only occasionally does some random convergence of gravity coax an asteroid from its orbit and send it tumbling on a new path, where it must either eventually find a new equilibrium on its own or die colliding with another body. A failure of this celestial harmony killed the dinosaurs, an overcoming of isolation that proved catastrophic. Isolation is the only assurance of safety.

Isolation seems safe, but it produces another kind of death. A population raised in isolation will eventually die off as genetics converge to paucity. A field sown with only a single crop will eventually become fallow as vital nutrients are depleted. With isolation, intellect withers; without movement, muscles atrophy, joints become less limber; we freeze. Calcification, petrification, occur when isolation overwhelms and some once-living thing becomes frozen in stone.

Turning inward, we turn to stone. Travelling outward is a risk, but the only assurance of growth. A wayward asteroid may find destruction, or it may find a new orbit all its own, unique. A bear slowly starves as it hibernates; if it never wakes and ventures out of its cave, it will die. A bird that never leaves its nest will never learn to fly.

On the wing, birdsong above. I stop to listen. A bird's song is danger and benefit, attracting the notice of both predators and potential mates. A bird that stays silent, that does not sing, stays safe, but isolated in its safety. And so it risks its song.

I stop to listen, and to look. The bird alights on a branch, exposed to danger and to risk, and adds its song to a multitude of others. I stand transfixed, and watch, in awe of its audacity. Nearby, you, with binoculars, watch as well, excited by the experience. Noticing me, you sing of this bird's song, of its specialness, its rarity. You tell me its name, its habits, the story of its long migration, your liquid eyes alight with the thrill of this encounter.

You offer me your binoculars, you hold them out. Hesitantly, tentatively, I reach out to take them. I look, feeling you breathless beside me, and your excitement begins to grow within me as well. I hand the binoculars back, thanking you, and our hands touch. We share a smile, happy at the ease of this random convergence of gravity.

In my mouth, a song begins to thaw.

I NEVER TIRE OF THE MOON STEPHANIE ROBERTS

A low sliver, silver they say. So long & good-bye
against the growing violet felt, it seemed to

hurt the sky by twin fire of emphasis and opposition.
Crescent, comma, scimitar, it was all of these things

& none. It was a seizure of the mind, it was:
time travel, extra sensory perception, aliens,

god's fallen lash, and Lucifer's lopsided smile flaming
down the night. I sent a prayer, *are you seeing this?*

Thankfully, we share the same sky if little else.
Fish shacks on a partially frozen river skirt

measured disaster. I wanted to run home along our
fault line, tell you all about it, like a bloodhound

retrieves a hare, lays it, noses the fork of your stance,
slobbers joy, hungry for my happiness.

THERE SHE GOES AGAIN SASHA BURSHTEYN

There she goes again,
pretending to be guava, to be gooseberry, to be
anything but fine mist
filling out a dress. She plaits
flowers into pigtail after pigtail, girl-child
after girl-child in crisp school uniform,
fingers smelling of jasmine; but
under her nails, a hint
of rot. Of sewage. Three canaries
where a heart should be, beating
their wings in tune to some stranger's
dusty whistling. She runs,
country to country, and still
beneath her skin the canaries rustle their way
north to south and back, and back;
they want what she wants without words:
the move, the go, the open sky, the out.

AS IF

GILL MCEVOY

As if we'd just turned the light off,
and silence had fallen,
you having had the last word.

As if any moment you might
rise, step into the dark garden
polishing the lens of your telescope
as you set it up;

as if the night-sky could cast again its magic,
we two counting constellations,
watching for shooting stars,

As if morticians were not so skilled
that they have you lying there
looking so alive
you might suddenly speak again.

As if it is possible to find the brightness
in the stars again.

GREY SKY, RAINDROPS ON THE WINDOW
RICHARD W. HALPERIN

Grey sky, raindrops on the window.
A letter from Japan on the table.
A dear friend distant and not distant,
We two by a stream,
Talking and not talking,
Smelling the smell that wet rocks make,
A volume of Montaigne nearby.
Two old dogs, mortality.
Young people walking by,
Splashing by,
We once.

Seen yesterday from a bus through Galway
A flock of birds lifting off from a field of brown heather.
Each bird a word.
The mass of them neither thought
Nor you.
But they were you.

Today a B&B in Greystones.
A letter from Japan on the table.
Letters.
Pens pushing forward
Montaigne, Madame de Sévigné
Conrad, Virginia Woolf.
Letters to friends.
Letters to the butcher.
Letters to old Uncle Dieter crippled in his chair.

Words lifting off.

THE WORKHOUSE — CLAIRE LOADER

It was Michael who died first. He was born from the weakness of my mother, frail, like a lonely tree windswept on the bog. You could see in her eyes, day after day, sorrow and pure exhaustion vying and pulling behind her dead, listless stare. Daddy didn't have the strength to bury him proper. Whisked by a fox from a shallow grave, our only comfort was that at least something had eaten that night.

It wasn't long before sickness came and took Colm too. He'd been the strongest of us all but it didn't seem to matter. I would often sit out alone on the path, twisting and turning the tatters of my skirt as the soft hues of day's end melted into twilight. The wagtail, so jolly at my feet, would head back to his nest and leave me with the stars, as one by one they crept out from the blanket of the sky, almost winking just at me.

I imagined them all to be angels, but it was hard to believe they could bear watching us all fall one by one. Watch as the fields lay fallow and the light of each cottage was snuffed out forever. There weren't many of us left now, the path quiet as I slowly slinked back home, the hard pads of my feet scuffing the dirt as I trudged up to the door. I knew it wouldn't be long now, the few scraps of dignity my parents had left were wearing thin. It was nearly time.

We weren't alone the day we finally conceded and made our way towards the village, our meagre possessions feeling heavy in our pockets. We were joined by more defeated souls on the slow march up the boreen, slipping out of the thicket like ghosts. No one said a word as we all slowly swayed up the track, like sheer blades of grass being softly blown from side to side, with so little as a wisp of skin keeping us from being lifted away.

We passed the walls of the grand house along the way, just able to spy the tall tower peeking out at us from above the surround. I'd never had a chance to go in; some I knew who served there, a lucky few not bound to the whims of nature, the blights and the scourges. I wondered, looking up at the tower, how the sky could still be so blue.

I'd only heard stories of the workhouse, my parents whispering at night in the light of the dying embers, whispering in fevered tones, hints of fear reaching me as I snuggled deeper into the blanket, trying desperately to forget the emptiness that gnawed inside my belly. It almost didn't register now, it was simply a new constant, one that held me close as we finally reached the main entrance and stood wavering at the gates.

They separated us when we eventually went in. Mammy didn't even cry as they led the men through a door to the right, and us off to the left. I never did see Dad again, his slow lanky figure my last memory as he shuffled through the door. They put all the women in the back block, the mess hall separating the men's yard from ours, dinner timed so we would never meet.

The younger children were sent to a separate block, away from the adults. The windows so high looking out onto the yard, that their mothers couldn't reach to see out. Although some still tried, desperately trying to hoist each other up on weak arms, just to catch a glimpse.

The nights were filled with moaning, broken only by a whimper, a cough. Mammy stopped talking altogether and it wasn't long until she just lay in the sleeping quarters, unable to go down to work in the laundry, just waiting to die. They buried her out in the field to the side of our block, a mound among many, a small pile of dirt pushing out from beneath the dandelions.

Life became a game of miserable repetition, filled with smells and sickness and death. I thought about the wagtail sometimes, mostly in the evening light, and wondered if he was still out in the meadow somewhere, flitting amongst the trees. I wondered if I would ever get out of here, or if I too was destined for the little field, where I could finally lie down and comfort my mother.

I slowed down the car, trying to peer inside the gap in the gate.

'Hey, what's that place, I wonder?'

'I dunno, it's not coming up on the GPS – do you wanna take a look?'

'Fuck it sure, why not?'

We pulled into the side of the road and parked in front of a small field. Several small rocks stuck out of the long grass, faint etchings indecipherable on their smooth, weather beaten surface. The rusty chain on the gate creaked and groaned as we edged the sides open and slid under the stone arch. A long, tall grey building ran down the left to meet the paddock below. Boarded-up windows and thick streams of ivy told of a structure long out of use.

We found an old side door down the far end, that sprinkled the ground with splinters and dust as we shoved and broke the rotting wood. Through a low tunnel, we emerged into a large square courtyard, enclosed on each side by a single-storey building to the right and a high wall to the left. A tall, four-storey building sat at the back, the wind whipping noisily through the missing tiles of the roof, like an old, tired orchestra. We jumped, trying to peer in through the windows, gaining flashes of broken wood, perhaps a table.

'Jesus, what was this place, do ya reckon? It's huge.'

'A school, I wonder? Maybe a factory?'

Our shoes sent up small showers of stones as we crunched our way over the yard, setting the crows to flight. They circled, cawing and cackling above the empty hollow buildings, their cries, like children screeching and playing, bounced off the walls to surround us in constant echo.

A movement to my right set my head to turn as a crow landed near my foot, cocking its beak in a curious stare before taking flight once more. I watched it heave its wings and fly over the wall into the field beyond, the thicket of tall grass and dandelions engulfing it from below. The courtyard suddenly felt cold; the dark, empty windows stared down at us, menacing. The wind picked up and, shivering, I hugged my jacket closer to my chest.

'Hey, you wanna get outa here? It's getting cold and this place is kinda creepy.'

'Ya, we should go. I'm getting hungry.'

MOTHERING SUNDAY AND A BLACKBIRD HAS ICE-CREAM ON ITS BEAK
ALICE WEST

Eyes, you are
a blackbird. Nose, you are his
beak. Gold and ink like a waking word,
poised to trace the treetops.

Feet, you are the last to leap aflight as
wings ignite in puffs of swaying
branch so only lacework leaves are left, and one loose
feather, lost for a passing child to find who'll call it a crow's

cape. Your cloak
fans out, knees in; you are the turning
of a page, a pianist's fingers scaling
roofs, legato, flapping

in concert dress and you
sweep the sky and land and sky and
spell a V of fellow wings in mass
For the Beauty of the Earth. Vibrato –

then the village oak to nestle;
notes of river, pollen, petrol, daffodils and how
you rescue a beetle, swallow him whole,
take off again

by noon. You want to swim in salty air and
sing your hymn, a single wave
back at the sea. So you flap
to Brighton Pier in time for tide out, little blackbird

You sole beast you brave fool you black bird

You watch me lick vanilla as I write.
I set the sun on my letter paper and gold nib, then
toss you the cone. You peck. And gone.
Tell my mother I love her.

COMBING THE HAIR ('LA COIFFURE') CIARÁN O'ROURKE

Edgar Degas, 1896. For my sisters

Days burn out; our inner life persists –
so this wall as red as a bursting fruit
could be a metaphor
for pain and sweetness both combined,
the easy, spreading wave of touch

a hairbrush tugs through all the room,
where soon you'll shindy from your seat
as the ritual completes, your hair
a flaring melody released
by the comber's tactful hands, her face

like yours a paragon
of second thoughts and soft abidance,
her deft, attending stance
the light
that sets your laughing arms aglow –

which leaves the watcher only
to depict, who keeps concealed
his stillness in the dance,
though every window's
singing now

his dream of praise, his passing glance.

SOUNDING 36
RAY MALONE

the place to get to   to be   to stare
back at where you were

there at the bend in the road

alone

the thread of an intention hanging in the air
to dare to go   to stay

the matter of the mind to be made

up to you to say

and the night descending

a stranger to yourself
to turn to home

or turn away

BETH

SUSAN MILLAR DUMARS

Ma says the bugs are back. Big ones this time. Tear shaped. They ooze. They're one place and then they ooze-drip to another place. They can move any which way. Across the table, down the wall, along the floor.

'Draw your knees in tighter. Tuck your shift between your legs. Mind they don't get in.'

I do what she says. Her eyes are jumping in her head. Looking here, looking there.

When she's like this, all nervy, it's like there's flames between us. Her face looks wavy like when you stare at the fire for too long. Her eyes are sparks and I can't touch her. I don't know why. She's right here, but it's like inside her skin, she's burning.

She whispers. Always whispers when she tells about the bugs. Like she's afraid they'll hear. Do bugs have ears? I don't know. I ain't never seen them. They don't show themselves to me. Ma says that's 'cos I'm a good girl.

She shows me where one of them pinched her. Right on the papery skin on top of her foot. 'They suck on you, and it feels like ice, and then like a proper hard pinch.' There's a little red mark. She starts to cry. Ernie's crying too, in his cot. Ernie's cries are just squeaks. He's not very strong.

The floor is cold. I wonder should I kiss her on the place where the bug pinched her. But I can't make myself do it. I have my arms tight around my knees and I'd like to close my eyes and let this all be a dream. But I can't. Her hair is in her eyes, she's crying, her eyes have cracks of red where they should be white. 'Beth,' she says. 'Beth.' Too close. Her face too close to mine and ugly with crying. Her breath. I'm knackered. I'll have to fetch the doctor. He's the only one can make the bugs go away. Back into the walls or wherever they go. Make them leave Ma alone.

'Beth!' Pleading with me. Nothing for it. I'll have to fetch the doctor.

All the lamps are lit. But there ain't no people. No horses. No barrels, baskets, carts. No shouting. No one rabbiting on. Just for a tic, I stand in the quiet. My fingers open up inside my pockets and I wish I could grab hold of this peace and keep it. No weeping. No faces raw red from tears. Just the smooth dark and the lamps like a row of cheerful little moons. All the houses sleeping. My breath makes clouds. And then the Bow Bells ring. One. Two. Three. Is it just one lad rings the bells? I don't know. I think of me and that lad and it's like we're on a ship by ourselves on a black sea. A great big ship called London. We can steer her wherever we like. I start to march real smart up the street, my shift sort of blooming white below my coat. I am Captain. Captain Beth says *stand straight!* Ring the bell, sharpish. Tell them we're on the way.

The last time there was blood. Beads of blood from nasty scratches up her arms. She'd been trying to flick the bugs off her. Dr Fitzgibbon whistled as he washed her arms and wrapped them in soft white bandages. That was after Ma drank the potion he gave her. The potion is the cure, it makes her sleepy and the bugs don't bother her no more. Dr Fitzgibbon said next time come to me before you see blood and get scared. Come to me when first she seems upset. I said I would and he said good girl. He has a big yellow moustache and his lips all pink and wet underneath. Good girl he said, and then he said she's right as rain much of the time so we'll try not to have her taken away. We'll try to care for her here. Understand? I didn't but I said I did. My heart went very fast. He gave me a boiled sweet from his pocket and patted my head.

Where would they take her away to? I reckon there must be a house somewhere, the far side of Mayfair maybe, where the walls are just walls. Not full of bugs inside, twitching, waiting. A clean house. Warm. I reckon Ma might like it there. But they mightn't let Ernie and me go too. They might say we're loud and messy and we don't belong in the clean house with Ma. Then I don't know what would happen. Thinking of this makes me run.

I run and run. The lamps blur to streaks of light. Like in a tunnel. The cold hurts to breathe. My legs pound. A tunnel that ends at the doctor's shop. Now I can see it. Just across the main street.

Then I'm in the air. Falling. I put out my hands but too late. The ground hits me. I make a noise, like 'Hunh.' My forehead, belly, knees. Something like waves going through me. Can't move. Then I do. I lift my head and turn it to one side. Through my hair, I see something close to my face. It's tall and thin and hard. Light shines cold off it. It's the end of a man's walking stick.

There's a cry that's not a cry. A growl. It has teeth in it. Then curses like the ones Pa's mates will shout as we're leaving the pub. Pa will say, 'Shut it. Lady present,' and grin down his arm at me and squeeze my shoulder and I give a little smile and they all laugh.

The same words. But nothing like laughter.

The walking stick disappears, and I feel a sharp whack on the back of my skull. I drop my head and cover it with my arms. Then kicks at my side. Then a terrible weight on me, on my back, it slams down on me again and again. I can't get air to scream. Then the weight is gone. I take a sudden, big breath, like coming up from under water. I'm choking on air and then I'm screaming, screaming, screaming.

After a time big hands turn me over so I'm looking at the sky. Something soft is tucked under my head like a pillow. There are faces over me. Dr Fitzgibbon closest, puffs of air coming out from under his moustache. 'Hush, child,' he is saying. 'Hush.' I didn't know I was screaming till he said that, it was a noise in my head but I didn't rightly know it was coming out of me. I go quiet then, just making little breath sounds like what Ernie does when he's fussy.

'Ooh, by Christ, that's a lot of blood. Can't stand the sight of blood, me.' That's Alice.

The doctor looks up with a small sigh. 'It's only her lip, m'dear. No cause for alarm. If you are feeling faint, please find a place to sit down. One patient is enough, thank you.'

But Alice is moving away, shouting. 'Here, Thomas! It's your Beth! Get over 'ere!'

The doctor is opening my coat, touching my arms and legs with quick, warm hands. 'Lie still, child. Let me have a look. Alright? Good girl.'

Nothing hurts. Everything hurts. My hair stuck to my face. My face feels wet. The sky is moving.

I hear running. Then Pa. His eyebrows bunched like caterpillars. 'Jesus, Beth! What the f—

'Keep a civil tongue in your head, sir.'

'That's my daughter! Don't you tell me – ' He rubs at his forehead with the back of his hand. 'She okay?'

'That's just what I'm trying to find out. She's –' Dr Fitzgibbon interrupts himself, looks up at Pa. 'Why have I never met you before?'

'Pardon?'

'I look after this girl's mother. Why have I never seen you in their home?'

Pa's shoulders go up. 'Don't live there, do I? She chucked me out. I live with Alice here, just down the laneway. Us and her sister, Margaret.'

I didn't know Margaret was here before Pa pointed her out. She's standing in shadow, arms across her chest, trying to hide that she's only in a nightgown. She's quiet, is Margaret.

Not like Alice. 'She don't look well to me at all. She looks halfway to heaven, poor mite.'

'Caught the villain!'

It's a new voice, and we all turn to see. A finely dressed man is standing with another, smaller man. He has the arm of the smaller one and is twisting it up behind his back. Alice and Margaret gasp. Pa's face goes a funny colour and he makes as if to punch the smaller man; it's Margaret who stops him, stepping in front of him and saying in her low voice, 'Tom, no!'

The doctor's hands, rebuttoning my coat, start to shake. I look up at his face. He's staring at the small man, and his face is gone funny. Like he might be sick. I never seen the doctor like that. He ain't the sort, know what I mean? He says, 'Dear God. Who is he?'

I turn back, to see what he's seeing. The little man's face is white in the lamplight. His skin looks so smooth and cold that I wonder does he have on a mask. He seems sort of stooped, yet not sickly or weak. No, upon my life, not weak. If he wanted to get out of the other man's hold, he could. Instead, he's laughing to himself. Laughing in a way that don't look like laughing. Clutched in his free hand is a walking stick.

He speaks. In a gentleman's voice, he says, 'Edward Hyde, sir. At your service.'

Pa and the women shrink back. From three separate people they turn into one shape. Dr Fitzgibbon suddenly takes off the dressing gown he's been wearing over his pyjamas and drapes it over me like a blanket. I try to catch his eye, but he's looking right at Mr Hyde. Like he's daring him to do something. Mr Hyde smirks.

The finely dressed man says, 'I saw everything. They ran into each other, the little girl and this. ... gentleman. She fell. And then he ... there is no other way to say it. He trampled over her. Like a stampeding animal, sir. *What have you to say for yourself, brute?*'

Mr Hyde, calm as you like, tilts and turns his head to look at me. 'The young lady should not be out, unaccompanied, at this desperate hour. It is a desperate hour, is it not? Where were you going, my child?'

I stare into his face and his skin starts to bubble. A layer of yellow fat shines under his flesh. His face darkens; his chin suddenly stretches long while his eyes become quite small. Tiny hairs shimmer on his jaw, his neck. I can't stand it. His black cloak seems to harden around him. I can't, can't. My teeth start to chatter.

Bug, I whisper. *Bug*.

DEAR FUTURE OCCUPANTS, — LAURINDA LIND

Sorry about the water in the cellar,
eventually it will seep away as it
always has done for one hundred
sixty years. You are living in the
middle of lakes that would love
to besot you from the bottom up.
Don't let the shivery bedroom shut
you down, either. All it needs is
heat generated between humans,
instead of the silent longing it has
soaked in for so long. Greet
the ghosts but keep going. They
are much more interested in
themselves than they are in you.
In summer it will stay cooler inside
than out due to all this stone,
which is a good reminder not
to let the neighbours get to you.
Experience says they will sail off
soon, seek new excitement,
and if you stay long you will add
another layer to all the time
ticking within these walls.

UNGEHEURES UNGEZIEFER — ANNE WALSH DONNELLY

After Franz Kafka

I didn't know I was in love
until yesterday. She sat
beside me at the board meeting
her hairspray mingled with mine
hem of skirt slid up her thigh
I wanted to touch her nude tights.

Today, I lie shackled in my husband's arms
his ramrod digs the small of my back
after-sex sweat blocks my pores
the memory of her kiss
imprinted in my mind.

My back stiffens,
skin darkens, belly domes,
splits into constipated-brown sections.
I have to manoeuvre myself out of bed
crawl towards the bathroom
scurry into the shower.

I didn't know being in love
would morph my body
into Kafka's *Ungeheures Ungeziefer*.

I let boiling water lash my vermin
armour. Cry cockroach tears
brown wings dissolve
antennae swirl down the drain.
Six spindly legs become two again.

I lie beside him, can't be with her,
if I'm to survive in this corporation
of pest controllers.

DEATH OF CUCHULAINN? — MICHAEL CASEY

Like the Pieta the statue is impossible;
at such an angle the body could not
be held by those bindings, sinews,
or by the sword-arm that circles the rock.
Generations of loss and fore-knowledge
of overwhelming force, too bravely dismissed,
strain for balance in the body's canted form.
Is there a flicker left to keep the fight alive,
as Prometheus tried to survive the rage
of gods made vengeful by his valour?
Despite the fearsome slumped head, a hero
does not die completely even when leached
of war frenzy or when the scald-crow leaves
the black cave and flies down to betray
with a wounding kiss of its tainted beak,
and sword and shield begin to slip from hands
and with them all inspiring urges of the heart.
Where the heroism in an empire winning?
The defeated know they cannot lose.
Was it mere drama to unveil the deeper truth
to watchers lining the road to Golgotha? Even so,
it will suffice if the promise of renewal holds.

MORNING ROOM   MARIA ISAKOVA BENNETT

Seven-thirty, September divided
between sunshine and shadow.
Through the window: the constancy of holly;
beyond: mossed brick, a quibble of buildings.
You're drawn back to the tick of the clock
though you never see the jolt of its hands,
back to the scent of a fire asleep
after last night's mad blaze, and back
to the objects that move only once or twice a year:
Grandma's bone china; a row of cups that say
Rutland Falls, Oban, and *Normandy cider*;
the table, its third decade, scrubbed,
no shine, variously naked, or covered in paper
or linen for birthdays, Christmas,
for dozens of *Welcome Home* meals,
and for one last meal before you leave.

THE TEA CEREMONY CLARE MCCOTTER

Standing at the open window, the green sleeves of her dress rolled up, her dark red lipstick smelling of summer dusk, she lights a cigarette and sending each exhalation high into the air lets the kettle boil until the thrush has emptied its throat. At the head of the stairs, his tall frame, wedged in a bedroom chair, waits. Three years since he was here, she couldn't hide the shock, seeing the shake in his hands, the pallor, the eyes full of thin ghosts and lilies. Wrapping a cloth round the kettle's iron handle she half fills the old brown teapot with boiling water. The men huddled in her hall all morning have spilled into the living room, one thinks he might speak, catching her eye he changes his mind. A chair scrapes the landing floorboards, starting a commotion beneath. Someone is shouting, 'Careful boys, careful'. Slamming the kitchen door and her eyes, she sighs, swishing water round and round and round the teapot's earthenware belly. Trying to remember the beginning, she wonders if it was always there; some small brittle thing inside, making him a little bit shier, a little bit more hesitant than the rest. Could it have been love, love winding him up like a prayer, winding him up too tight, until something had to give? She hears them muttering; they are talking about a plan. She cups her hands around the teapot letting its warmth seep into her skin. They say no-one has ever seen him drop a tear, neither as boy or man, not a single tear shed, but they could say the same about her, not a tear shed, even when the long evenings crush her like a rose.

Taking her back to Glasgow the long evenings always make her sad. For there is something about a day stretching out across a couch of stars that makes her think of that cobbled Glaswegian street, the splattered light and the noise and the great dray horses; the only harvest a crop of children's faces, hatching houses and hospitals and shops from tin cans and brush shafts and stones. Still home, the lanky grey-stone tenement where a boy lay on a settle bed, his flimsy ribcage snatching at every passing breath until consumption shook it quiet, later folding her parents' arms across their chests. And still home, the mother tongue taken away but never forgotten, watered with each trip back to bruised footpaths she lost at five years old, her and Michael and little Mary brought to this big house full of women. Too sad to feel the gentleness that rocked them to sleep in sun-bleached sheets, she longed for the tenements, for her mother's voice mingling among the voices of her neighbours, for gaslight, for smog, for the city's tireless soul. The house she came to own becoming home to a husband, a daughter, and a son, to her sister long after she had gone, but never really home to her. She flings the water into the sink, adds another strone from the kettle, swishing it round and round in the opposite direction. They are still whispering. One of them mentions 'a catch'. Thinking you couldn't catch a cold, she feels at sea. The chair moves again, and someone shouts, 'Holy Christ'. She is at sea, maybe she always is; maybe home is a ferry somewhere between Larne and Cairnryan. She knows it was the stretch in the evenings, the change in the clock that brought him back. The kitchen door opens, nodding in her direction, a man from Antrim says, 'If you're planning on going up there forget it, this situation needs to be handled with the utmost caution.'

A spark flies from the corner of her eye. Green and flinty, her eyes could start a fire, but behind the green and flint there are tug lines, and maps, and one small bobbing paper boat. Emptying the teapot again she opens a wooden caddy, measuring out black tea leaves on the palm of her hand. She wonders if she should have seen it coming; the changes had been there. But how could anyone have anticipated that?

He had always been a bit different, lugging round those old odds and ends, broken plates, shelves, shoes, jam jars, anything broken, anything with a fracture, anything with a crack needing a thin silvery lining of glue. No harm in that, no harm in this man, mild-mannered as May. Distracted at times to be sure, standing alone, he seemed to hear voices on the wind, petitions rising up from the river grasses, prayers in the leaves coming down, but never, she thought, never answered back until Arthur died in his twenty-first year. The kettle splutters. She moves it off the heat, lets it settle for a moment, and pours it over the tea. After Arthur died it really began, all that talk, saying he could live the boy again, nothing needed only a battery and a song. So sure, so sure he could live his brother again that it took five to drag him out of the graveyard, his heart smashed to pieces, the look on his face as they took him away imprinted on the back of her brain. Two years under lock and key before he settled; if that's what you call it when medication douses out your fire. Moved to an open ward he seemed half content until the lengthening of the light opened up the possibility of the road. That stretch in time reminding him of his two fields, long and thin like dress sleeves; spring stoking the soles of his feet till he could sit in the big dusk-filled dayroom no longer. Time after time, slipping quietly out of the ward and out of the grounds, he headed in the direction of the Largy Line. Contacted by the nurse in charge his cousin would meet him walking head down between the hawthorn hedges, and for a day or two he would visit, always seeming content enough to go back. This time was different. Pressing on the lid of the teapot with her fore and middle finger, she pours a little, before leaving it to amber on the heat's edge.

This time he came home, not to his cousin's house, but to his own dusty boards at the crossroads. His sister, back from New York, had cleaned and scrubbed and said she would stay. Too soon talk turned to Arthur, turning her head with all that business about living him again. Then he said if she happened to die, he could live her too. Seeing him slip further into the wind and the leaves and the grasses, she became afraid, ringing the hospital when she saw him carrying a car battery from the shed. Two nurses came in a taxi. They talked for a while; he agreed to return, and excusing himself for a second slipped out the back, slipping straight in her front door. Michael's shotgun was in its usual place. He loaded it and climbed the stairs. She checks the tea; it is drawing nicely. He had been restless since he came back. She could see it, no happier here than in that ward full of old men, sleep still in their eyes at noon, fingernails brown with nicotine and neglect. Neither here nor there, home had changed. Maybe some people never have one, she thought. Maybe for some it is a stretch of road, a stretch of road long and black in the lengthening light. Opening the cabinet door she lifts down a big white breakfast cup and saucer, rinsing both under running water. She wonders what they will say to him; what will they do if they get him to go back ... observe, medicate, return him to a ward where everything is time, where there is a mountain of time and time for nothing ... the quick wash, the quick shave, the quick word, the clock in the heart of it all, the routine hewn in granite. She pours the tea, adds milk and placing a teaspoon on the saucer wipes the rim. Would that routine become his home, at twenty-seven years of age would he pull it round his shoulders close and warm as a dark evening? Holding the saucer between her thumb and forefinger she climbs the stairs, and whispering four words lifts the gun from his lap, filling his hands with all the time in the world brimming in a white cup.

CLEANING THE LABYRINTH — LAUREN CAMP

At near night, without stars,
agree to the spiral:
one breath,
then another.
Let the moon change
colour. The route
is an arrangement
of organised struggles. No one
to see you tripping over.
This afternoon, long winds punished
cottonwoods, clipped heavy limbs
and flung them to maze.
Kick them aside, loving best
the next turn. To rid
the circle of flux, bend
and throw branches from the round.
(Otherwise, I am not here
with myself.) Step again to enter
and withdraw from the middle.
A labyrinth is for calming
the breach. It takes a long time
for redemption or something
similar. Stacked pebbles
embellish the dust. Walk without
thinking, steady and quiet. Hear
upraised tree limbs. Hear wind
without logic direct
one possible way.

LOVE ME ANYWAY   KORY WELLS

And these are my vices:

Envy, sloth, sugar   butter, salt, sweet

   wine in screw-top bottles, cheap

sparkly jewellery and saying yes   to every good cause

     and even some lost ones.

And how I dance gracelessly

   and abandon novels too easily

   after the first climax   and drift from my sentences

   especially in the bleary mornings

     after late nights strumming

song after song   till my fingertips ache.

And how I'm not bold enough

   to always speak for all that's right

not faithful enough   to believe in the power of prayer

   more than I believe in

   the curve of my hips because

as I already said: Sugar.

Your lips. Your voice.   The way my insides quicken.

   How even though it irks you

      I never close the pantry door

the packages perched inside   bright birds that sing

   our paradise, and I'm hungry

   always hungry for more.

WHERE ARE WE GOING   KARLA VAN VLIET

Toward north, to ice-cover and sky
both light and white and blinding.

Cutting down to dark waters we mark
our passage with a rift into depths,

into dark breathing, whale body, walrus,
tides. And memory; aloneness turned cold,

I am lonely. All horizon is thin line. I have
cast, float and sinker: these words

scribbled into posts. I unfold them
into wind. Sea swallows lift and turn.

ATLANTIC LEATHER CO.

DOUGLAS W. MILLIKEN

She came for me again last night. Stood in my kitchen and told me to join her. Told me everything would be fine. Scarf wrapped high and tight on her neck. It made her small mouth smaller. She told me: everything will be okay.

The club. There were friends already at the club. An army is stronger than a soldier. X and Y were there. And everyone else. Amid burnt-black wood and soft light rendered of gold. The compliment in every server's smile. Everything so loud you didn't have to hear. I drank so I believed I was just like everyone else. So aren't I everyone else now? X touched my hair and Y touched my clothes. My skin became public domain.

Yet I went home alone after that. Hungry. Poured another drink. Lit only one kitchen light. Waited for it to speak. But waiting makes me anxious. All my doors are old and strong. But some must be stronger than others. The bedroom. I took off my belt in the room's cool dark and circled it around my neck. Tossed the rest over the door and then closed the door. Then I just relaxed. Let the belt hold my weight. Relaxed. The darkness became more fluid like paint. Then other pictures were there. Scarves and rendered gold. I pushed my feet into the floor before I could pass out. Breathed. Drank the air. A warm unfocused fuzz of fresh blood welcomed home my brain. It felt good. I was happy. I'd been one place before. Now I was somewhere else.

People talk about time travel. They don't know this is what they mean.

Later, smoking outside in the rain, the fear finally overcame me. Never before had I been so close. Reach for it. Touch nothing. There are street lights blurring through the water that falls. But they won't speak to me now. I shake until the rain turns to snow. I know this is wrong. But tell me what's right. She comes and goes and I stay here. Why didn't I go further?

There is no one I can talk to about this.

EVEN A MONKEY   LISA C. TAYLOR

When he whacked the top of the clock to stun the Zen flute music into silence, I was in a half-sleep, the kind where covers felt like swaddling and the breeze sent a delicious shiver.

'Don't forget your meeting with Jessup.'

Thomas is my timekeeper, punctual to a fault while I meander through my ablutions, nicking myself with the too-dull razor, noticing a line of shaving cream still on my face. I hate shaving because it's a ritual. Only when we are on vacation do I let the shadow on my face roughen until Thomas runs his hand over it with his smooth fingers, fingernails clipped and clean.

'You need a shave, man.'

I didn't mind placating him. In exchange, I get to live in a townhouse with a king-sized bed and velvet draperies, and maid service. Weekend getaways to the mountains or seaside are important to Thomas and I enjoy those times as well. He asks little of me other than I keep clean, faithful, and practise good dental hygiene.

'Have you ever thought of modelling, Lee?'

I ruffle his perfect hair; pull my face into an unassuming pose.

'Nah. I would hate everyone looking at me.'

I know he's smiling because he relishes having me to himself. It's part of the story he's built, that I am unaware of my looks. If I could sell the names of men who have told me that, I'd retire.

Years ago when Pop took us out of Boston and we never again lived in one place; I got a taste for awakening to cardboard sunsets on hotel walls and highway exit signs. I'd ride up front with him while Sadie worried the upholstery in the back.

'Where we goin', Pop?'

'Ah, Sadie-sugar, we're on an adventure. Gonna see the wide world. Don't you want your Pops to have opportunity?'

Sadie didn't answer because we both knew that opportunity often came in the form of a series of women sharing the bathroom with us, and leaving dirty dishes in the sink. Pops had no taste in partners, which I fortunately did not inherit. Our Mama died of meningitis so we were stuck with him. I couldn't wait to grow up.

Thomas pushes me out the door but not before he kisses me twice, fills my travel cup with my favourite pour-over Mexican single-origin coffee and hands me a homemade lemon poppy seed muffin. He says I look like Ryan Reynolds, once voted *People* magazine's Sexiest Man of the Year. I return his kisses; feel his gym-toned biceps. I know that he wants to make me into a better person. Under his tutelage, I can now choose a good wine, order with a passable accent at a French restaurant.

'You'll do fine, Lee. Just be yourself.'

Bad idea. Prospective employers want to see an image of what they think they're looking for. My job is to convince them that I am a lab assistant. I'm a poor worker, not even passable, being lazy and forgetful by nature. But Thomas believes in me and since we've only been a couple for eight months, I don't correct this delusion.

Pop called last week from La Conner, Washington.

'Got a job as a bartender in this cool bar with licence plates all over on the wall. You should visit. The writer Tom Robbins lives here. Didn't he write some crazy shit?'

Yeah. Shit about a hitchhiking woman with a huge thumb. Used to read his books after I took whatever chemical concoction was popular. Pop is neutral about my sexual orientation, sometimes seeing it as a way for him to prove how open-minded he is and sometimes telling me to tone it down.

It's a lot to live up to, being the gay son. I try to fit the stereotype whenever I visit, wear tight jeans and a designer shirt, add dips and peaks to my speech. It nearly always gets him going. Most of the towns Pop chooses are end-of-the-road truck-stop kind of places. One bar. One diner. Men in stained polyester shirts perched on bar stools drinking cheap see-through beer.

I sip from my travel mug and bite into a muffin that isn't the slightest bit dry. How does he do that? Thomas is better than most. My last boyfriend had this tattoo addiction. I didn't know that was a thing until

Miles. Apparently one or three isn't enough and these people want every inch of their body covered with snakes or Chinese symbols. I couldn't get past the green and blue skin. It looked less like art and more like a disease. But Thomas is unblemished, just trots off to the law firm in a Dior suit with a grey silk tie. Still, it's time I pushed off. I hate to overstay my welcome, have him bitching about Jessup and how a monkey could have gotten the job he set up. Even a monkey has his limits.

I drop my tie and cell phone in the bin by the railway station; buy myself a ticket to Anacortes, Washington. Usually I stay about ten days; just long enough to go to the library and look up the next place I might want to be. Sure, I'll miss his clean smell and the way servers ran around trying to please him but the two good suits and five designer shirts in my duffle will be the key to my new story – burned-out hedge fund manager or former CEO. No way to tell Thomas that a year and a half at a community college didn't make me a lab assistant.

See what happens when you trust a monkey? Monkeys steal, even from their fathers. Still I'm welcome to eat his food and crash on his couch for the time it takes me to find a place where I can be someone else. I'll start with that hotel with the cardboard sunset on the wall, then find a man in Levi's and Tony Lama boots, a man who isn't afraid to get his hands dirty.

RISING

VINNY STEED

I
am the ears of a sugar plant
strained, hearsay of leaves
earth-arrhythmia
I am the tiller of dreams.

I
am a foreign language
grounded, small syllables forged
in darkness, root-rumblings
a secret softly woken.

I
am the gutter-seed
emboldened, nestled on the back
of larvae, root and giant
grub. I am star-searching.

I
am sapling
opened, shooting for words
born of clay and air
I am stalk-stuttering.

I
am tree-bearing
rising pool of noise, vocal fibres deep
Listen to the roar of my stomata
Branches chattering with the gods.

SISYPHUS IN PARADISE   MICHAEL DERRICK HUDSON

I did nothing to deserve this; I just walked away.
The gates were unlocked, the guards

with their pitchforks skedaddled, demoralised
and unpaid, paperwork shredded

and all their absurd passwords
forgotten. Albert Camus drifted off years before,

my only fan, sipping espresso from a fragile cup,
ashing Gitanes with delicate fingers,

jotting in his diary: *I just got so bored.* I miss it

in a way. After a few centuries you grow fond
of the boulder, its cool little dimples

and fissures pressing again and again against

your hell-scorched cheek. I liked the implacable
bulk of it, its undefeatableness,

how sheer inertia's more than enough to pull you

apart. I miss getting patched up by those nurses
in the Dispensary, their skilled,

dutiful hands putting things right for another few
centuries. At first, Zeus came down

to gloat. Then he grew ironic, then cynical, then,

I don't know – sad? Envious? He brought me
new shoes, a second-hand wineskin

full of Heaven's best. He'd suggest I knock off

early and have a nice weekend. After a while it
wasn't a request. I'll never

admit this on my résumé, but I think I got sacked ...

GOLDEN BOUGHS

MARY O'BRIEN

Like divers, they have plunged in,
adjusted their sight to an otherworld,
happy to allow the incongruity,
the mismatches, the absurdity of it all,
how things arise, take form,
disappear again.

The Big Bang still spews gasses,
planets form and speed through green space,
storms are swirling across oceans, calm-eyed;
the centre of the web is dark and from it
they come crawling, all things various.

Snakes and mermaids swim together,
here an owl, there a goblin who has lost an eye,
wombs are opening, bonds and bounds
are formed and broken.

Charon plies his dark trade on the Styx
and Odysseus still sails for home.
Dazzling neurons spark and crackle
in the human brain and a town turns festive
as fireworks spill their colours
through the early winter dark.

Such lovely madness
and easy to fall victim,
find you haven't got a leg to stand on

but trusting in their golden boughs,
a brush, the pen, they have come through,
finding more than just a leg to stand on –
see there, a ballerina has emerged,
someone has found a way to dance.

COMING OF AGE

ELLEN DENTON

They're going to slaughter the chickens one by one. Mama says that with papa laid up with two busted legs, there's no way around it. There's no money for food, so one of the milk cows and all the chickens except for two good egg layers have to go – that it will give us the meat we need to get through the winter.

I told mama I would get a job after school. I can babysit or maybe find something part time in town, but she says no one is going to hire a fourteen year old to do anything that will pay enough to get us by till papa is back on his feet, not with a family of six.

They don't see the farm animals as living things in the same way that I do. Sometimes I go to the barn and look into their eyes and see something that's the same as me inside, but dressed in the skin and bones of a cow, or I'll pick up one of the hens when it comes up to the porch steps to greet me, and I can feel its heart beat against my arm right through the feathers, the way I can feel my own when I press hard on the skin covering my chest.

I don't want them to die, so I've spent all afternoon thinking of ideas on how to come up with enough money to feed us all and pay for the other things we'll need, but none of them will work.

Except for maybe one, but if I do that, I don't know how I'll be able to live with myself after, let alone explain to my parents how I got the money.

*

Grandma lives with us in a little bedroom on the second floor of the house. She owns a ring with a big diamond in it because she'd been married to a very wealthy man. He's been dead for twenty years though.

Six years ago, she came to live with us because she was no longer fit to take care of herself. Her jewellery and other valuables had already been sold by that time, except for that one ring. She would never let go of it because it meant a lot to her. She said it was a special token of love from the best years of her marriage and her life.

I could take the ring and sell it somewhere and it would give us more than enough money to get by. Grandma, long ago when she showed it to me, told me how much it was worth and even had the old, yellowed receipt from the store that it was bought from. Now she wouldn't even know if it was gone because she's not right in the head anymore.

Her room is below the attic, and she says all the time that there are people walking around up there – that she hears them laughing and singing – that they took the model train set she had eighty years ago as a child and they play with it up there – that she can hear it running around and around on the tracks.

Sometimes she tells me a story, and then tells it again ten minutes later, because she can't remember having told it once, or she'll call me by a name that belongs to someone else.

There's no one in the attic though and no train or tracks. She won't know if I take the ring, because she herself can't remember where it is now, and it's only fair the money from selling it gets spent for food and what not. Papa has been supporting her since she moved in, and mama and all of us girls have been doing for her too, as she can't do for herself anymore. I know stealing is a sin, but I've cared for those chickens from the time they hatched, and the cow they're fixing to slaughter I raised myself since she was a calf.

I know where grandma hid the ring because I saw it once when I was cleaning her room.

*

I have it in a bag under my mattress now. Tomorrow is Monday, when the jewellery store I had planned to go to with it will be open again, but now I think I'll have to return it to its hiding place in grandma's room.

I haven't been able to think up any way to explain where the money came from if I did sell it except to admit what I did. Mama and papa have always said that things like stealing and lying are some of the worst things a person can do – that they shrivel the soul and stay with you ever after, even if you try to forget about having done them.

I thought about maybe just telling them the truth so that at least I wouldn't have to make up a lie about how I got the money, but I saw grandma a little while ago, and now I don't think I can go through with it at all.

I brought lunch up to her on a tray and looked at her sitting in the bed. She always looks so shrivelled and small, her face so pinched and stitched with wrinkles, her eyes so dull and sad, but she smiled when I approached her with the food. Her eyes fixed on the tray when I came into the room and they followed its path all the way to the bed until I placed it on her lap.

I looked around at her room which is as drab and sad as she is, with hardly any furniture in it and not even nice pictures on the wall, just a drinking glass with daisies in it that I put there yesterday to brighten her day. I felt extra bad though when I realised that things will never get better for her. She will not get well or have fun or exciting things to look forward to in the future, There won't even be nice furniture brought in to fix up her room because there's never extra money for things like that. That ring is all she has left of what was once a good life, plus, if she hadn't birthed papa, who then sired me and my younger sisters, we wouldn't even be here today with whole lives of our own to live and futures to look forward to.

I'm going to return the ring to her – not back into its hiding place, but right into her hands so that she can see it and touch it again.

*

Mama slaughtered the first of the chickens this morning and after removing the head and feet, handed it off to me to pluck the feathers so it's ready for dinner roasting.

I felt a badness about it that I could not even put into words, but mama saw it in my face and understood. She told me to think of the good that will come out of it. She has often told me, when a bad thing happens, to think of how it may change me for the better – how heartbreak can sometimes even aim you like an arrow onto a new path in life you hadn't thought to go.

I didn't have much time to dwell on that though as I was already running late for catching the school bus and still had to get washed up and dressed in clean clothes.

I did, and then ran all the way across our field. The bus arrived before I got to the road, but instead of driving on, it stopped and sat there because the driver saw me running like mad with my book bag hanging over my shoulder, flapping against my side. People are nice like that sometimes.

On the ride to school, we passed the usual fields and farms, tractors at work and at rest, and herds of grazing cattle and sheep – sights so commonplace to me I barely even notice them anymore coming and going from school, even when my eyes are facing outward through the window in their direction. Today though, I did see them sharp and clear as cold creek water.

I think now that I'd like to be a veterinarian when I get out of school.

*

Tonight, when I brought grandma up her dinner tray, she smiled girlishly, almost like a mischievous little child, put her hand beneath the covers, pulled out the diamond ring to show me, then quickly shoved it down into the blankets again. She doesn't have a fun future to look forward to, but when I placed that ring in her hands last night and folded her fingers around it, it was like she had found her way back to the world of a happier past when there was still much to hope for, and I have never seen her look so young nor her eyes so shiny-bright.

UNLEAVING

RUTH THOMPSON

Years and years I've come to you
like this – sliding in to touch base,
dirt in my teeth.

Years and years I've leaned against you,
breathing. Green skin, sap-stuck,
fissured as mine is now.

You wore willow
and I climbed up weeping.
You put on god tree when I needed gods.

Still, it's strange to find you waiting,
back here where we began.
Years and years round to the smell

of dust and tannin – as if this life
I've made so much of
were nothing but a squirrel's

flimflam. Once I fell
through a vortex of spinning
aspen leaves.

It's taken me a lifetime
to know the place
for home.

STALLED CHILDHOOD — OKWUDILI NEBEOLISA

It was just after the rain, we sat
listening to the water drip from the roofs
into buckets kept at their hem waiting
like the beggars who lined St Joseph's walls
hoping that faithfuls would be moved to offer.
Slowly the muddied world came out of its shell,
the rain had already shortened the day,
stalled us in our bungalows, walled our childhoods,
even the butterflies, the moths, their wings
were barely proofs of the world outside.
September rains were endless, we mostly slept
through the percussion and woke to a bruised world –
the sky would have bled all its deep purple.
My mother would say *picture yourself*
in the ground, uncertain whether the earth
would be greedy enough to swallow you,
a ruckus outside, that was my childhood.
Whenever there was something strafing
in the sky, we had to run inside,
underground, sometimes a whole family
was buried in that way with their regrets.
I had heard this story before, always
it was incomplete, and we always knew
how it would end, our mother's little sermon
anytime people talked about the war
and how another could 'repair' the country,
her complete disbelief, she could never
forget the memories of hunger, the man
with the empty sleeve who was full of jokes,
the nurses who had cried bringing him to life,
perhaps he was now a beggar, the name

he used to call her. *And now another war?*
Hearing younger people rehash how
another war could be the solution
in obfuscated ideologies, it was
as if everyone else had broken a vow.
How could people not see an empty field
and cherish it, all that space for flies to mate,
like a day partly entered into,
my mother turning the questions to me,
asking, Dear what has gone wrong with the world,
what is it with their taste for oblivion?

FINDING MADRID EAMON MC GUINNESS

7th February 2010

Snow is covering the tops of distant mountains.
Where is this metropolis? My route home.
Brown Spanish earth below,
the villages don't look real.
You said you'd come for me,
come to Madrid Airport to hold me.
I can't find Madrid.
I can't find my father.

I want to tell him I received an e-mail from an old college lecturer.
I want to tell him I'm in love.
I want to tell him how much I enjoyed staying up late
with him and the lads over Christmas.
I want to tell him I'll look after Sinead.
I want to tell him I love him.
I want to tell him
We've passed the mountains,
the seatbelt sign is on,
(I want to tell him)
that
somebody has found Madrid,
somebody has found Madrid.

AMATEUR ESCAPOLOGISTS — JOHN WALL BARGER

'I love you, Mandy,' I said, kissing her belly button. 'Brandy,' she said. 'Tell me everything, Brandy,' I said. 'I have a kid named Kandy,' she said. She opened her wallet to a photo of a tomboy in a striped baseball cap, big smile, front tooth missing. 'Leave her. Run away with me,' I said. Brandy cried & cried. We climbed on a bus. For years we lived in harmony. Brandy delivered mail for the Post Office. I waited tables at a diner. Each evening we met at the diner for burgers. We sat in a booth & read letters Brandy had stolen. I held up a foolscap page teeming with tight red loops & read, 'With you I climax with such outrage as to stitch a caesura in the pulsebeat of the world.' We laughed & tore it to bits. Brandy found a greeting card. HAPPY BIRTHDAY, it said. Inside was written, in wobbly old-world script: 'You are quite unnecessary, young man!' A ten-dollar bill floated out. We ordered milkshakes. Then Brandy was sobbing. She was holding an envelope that said 'Toof Ferry.' No note, just a tooth that bounced out onto Brandy's ketchup, boulder in a lake of blood. We climbed on a bus. Kandy lived in a tiny unpainted house at the edge of town, near a tent city of homeless vets. Brandy ran ahead to the door & banged on it. Brandy herself answered. Brandy stared at Brandy. They even had on the same clothes: jeans, red boots, Mardi Gras beads, sailor's caps. Inside-Brandy said, 'Have you heard the roar of the sea?' Outside-Brandy said, 'The woods are riddled with paths, untold ways out.' 'Long live the day!' said Brandy. 'Long live the day!' said Brandy. They hugged. Outside-Brandy walked in, calling, 'Kandy-cane!' Inside-Brandy walked out, kissing me softly. We climbed the fence & walked through the derelict village of vets toward the bus station.

ANIMAL — ALISON MCCROSSAN

The men are closing in on Joe. Woods filter sunlight into blades. Beneath him is the ground, but it pitches skyward before him. Shouldn't he have gone for the river? The flap of a bird's wing somewhere above mocks him.

He's a pristine animal. Veins ripped and wasted into a bloody blur, but free for two days running. No drugs taken. There's a teardrop on his brain. Freedom isn't supposed to unfold like this.

Joe knows he's a junkie, else how could he feel like this? Torn to pieces by need.

The summit is rock, with sparse tree growth. There's nowhere left to go. It's the crest edge, to throw himself over, or the hunters.

He knows how to hunt. Score.

He spent the morning in the blistering sun just to burn away his apathy, though it was a cold winter day and the sun was a scraggly beast that offered little warmth but scratched the eye.

Hardly time to make amends now, tick tick tick. He owes twenty thousand and they want it in flesh. Each in turn. He knows the score.

Would it be so bad to die? Another day he'd believe he'd fly off that edge, the mountain-top. He'd done the usual things junkies do: blowjobs to strangers, sitting on concrete with a paper cup at his feet, threatening his mother, neglecting his son. Money from dealing would change everything, he'd thought. He's a junkie and does what junkies do; mismanaging his trades, misjudging his tabs. And now the men want their twenty thousand euro.

The sky above is icy. A cloud pattern visible here and there.

There's a rag on the branch of a stark black-barked tree. The branch is gnarled and the rag is blue, pale.

He runs to the rag. It's just a rag.

He falls to his knees. Clawing for a sign. What was he expecting? Something to grasp. A word from God?

There's a footprint in the mud before him and another, leading to the edge.

He crawls along the track of prints.

There's a path, a rugged rocky affair, descending.

Dreams tear at his eye: a night's sleep, a child's dance. He's tripping on terror; he's running out of space.

Was it a morning ago? He'd crumpled on the street, hand out for relief. Grubby, soiled, insular, derelict, he sat in a ball against the hurtful grey block of a Cork city building.

A boy passed, hanging off a balloon. Was that his son? Was that a feeling?

A bird calls out. He tells himself, listen for the song. A boy's word. A mother's murmur.

But streets will beckon, mad men will pursue.

He'll flee. He'll flee and fall, fall, fall into space.

Twenty thousand falls.

Pristine animal.

MY VIEW OF THINGS

KEVIN HIGGINS

after Edwin Morgan

What I love about lateness is the hope
I might get to slip off home before you turn up.
What I hate about punctuality is always getting there
in time to chat before you leave.
What I love about angle-closure glaucoma
is not seeing you
when you're standing right in front of me.
What I hate about comebacks
is the possibility you'll have one.
What I love about impotence is the sight
of you jiggling your bits at me in the hope I might
review your book/pretend to like your poetry/remember
your name, and it having no effect whatsoever.
What I love about my chronic lung condition
is the hours of enforced sleep during which I can dream
of a world in which I've never heard of you.
What I love about going slowly deaf
is not being able to hear the television.
What I love about nuclear holocaust
is the TV studio, in which those three men
are agreeing with each other, will no longer exist.
What I love about Crohn's disease
is the hours I spend on the toilet,
during which I miss comedy panel shows
in which Alan Davies talks to Alan Davies
about Alan Davies. What I love about your likeable face
is my ability, most days, to see past it.
What I hate about you wondering why Trump won
is your failure to look in the mirror.

What I love about memory is remembering
your rhetorical question:
How many Palestinian publishers are there?
What I love about dementia is the chance to forget
you once, very briefly, existed.

THE MEANING OF THE DOG DIGGING IN THE GRASS
LAURA FOLEY

Same as the hill quiet with dark green pines,
the air rent by a crow's screeching,
the woodpecker's tap-tap-tapping into a hollowed tree,

same as the green clover sprig rising from a new-mown field,
a purple flower emerging after autumn frost,
feathers of milk weed seeds releasing into flight,

same as a poplar tree's silver shimmering in wind –
the cloud come to cool the skin of a human
sitting cross-legged on the grass, breathing oneness in.

LOSING SIGHT   JEAN TUOMEY

Imagine never seeing a harvest moon again,
illuminated disc on an Autumn evening,
or mist lying low on a midlands farm
as the early train chases towards the day,
or starlings twist in shadows before dusk,
wheeling stunts as they whirl before roosting,
or fields rolled out, ready to sow,
bog black, smooth as an untossed bed,
or clouds, pink edged, sink into the sea,
floating ribbons that trim the horizon.

Moments that tip the scales;
a child is ill, a parent falls,
a friend brushes off
another black eye,
a building collapses
in Aleppo.

Imagine a haze,
a murky sky,
a dense fog,
not even
one bright
star.

AND I WILL COME RUNNING — JOE DAVIES

The media were on about the eclipse for days before it happened. I assumed I'd miss it, since I usually do. Then, on the actual night, when clouds covered most of the sky, I said to myself, 'See? I knew it'd be something.' I also wondered why anyone cared. Once you've heard the explanation for what's happening, once you've seen it a couple of times, what is so fascinating? It was a mystery, now it's not. Now it's an occasional reminder of how little we once knew – and also, surprisingly boring to watch. That I feel mildly cheated whenever I miss one is nearly as interesting.

On the night of the eclipse I agreed to meet up with my sister. This time she was going to do it. She was really going to leave her husband. She needed my support. She wanted my ear. There was nothing wrong with her marriage except that the two of them were wrong for each other. I could have said something before she married, but I didn't. Others tried. There was no violence, no outward sign of disagreement, just three years of complete and utter lack of compatibility. She liked spending money they didn't have, he liked watching basketball. There was no middle ground where they could meet. And as far as I could tell, there was no spark.

To be honest, I was getting tired of it. This happened about three times a year – my sister's panic, her going on about feeling like she was suffocating – and it never led to anything, because there was one way my sister and her husband were exactly alike. Both worried what others would think. Which was ridiculous. Everyone knew their marriage was ill-fated, that it wouldn't last, but somehow, having to admit to making a mistake was worse than living with it.

I'd agreed to meet her at one of the cafés downtown, the more expensive one of course. On the walk there I kept looking up at the clouds, gauging the chances of seeing anything. Sometimes I caught glimpses of the moon, at other times it was only a bright patch in the clouds. Mostly I saw nothing.

Growing up with my sister had its moments. Six years younger than me, she was more like the family pet, with about as much expected of her. There are only the two of us. I can remember being the one who held her hand whenever we went anyplace busy, being the one who watched over her at the park. The time she ran away it was my fault. Actually, it was never clear whether she deliberately ran away or just wandered off. We'd been at the park, which was next to a ravine. I'd been hanging from the monkey bars, revelling in how absurdly good I was at going back and forth. When I looked over at the sandbox where my sister was meant to be, she was gone.

I looked everywhere. Down the three paths into the ravine, up and down the road. There was no sign of her. I ran home to break the news and the search began in earnest after that. I was to blame. The way things grew quiet around me was how I knew. Hands fell on my shoulder. Heads shook. Nobody slept. When she was discovered the following morning inexplicably asleep at the foot of my bed there followed an explosion of all the emotion that had been pent up for the previous seventeen and a half hours. It had been unbearable. It was over, but it seemed forever before things returned to some kind of normal, and my sister never explained to anyone's satisfaction what she'd done with herself, where she'd been or why. The cost to me was never compensated nor acknowledged.

Three blocks from where I was headed, the moon finally broke through the clouds. It was full and bright and seemed larger than usual, and I was fairly sure that the dark smudge at one edge was the beginning of the eclipse. Every few paces after that, I glanced up. The clouds briefly got in the way again, but by the time I'd reached the café the moon was completely unobscured by clouds. I stood a moment and looked at it before stepping inside.

I was a couple of minutes late but there was no sign of my sister. This was typical. I went to the counter and got myself something, then took a table near the door. At first I wouldn't admit to myself why that table, but a little later, when my sister still hadn't shown up, I saw that what I wanted was to be free to step out easily and check the eclipse's progress, which I did several times. I wasn't the only one. All along the sidewalk stood people in twos and threes, their heads tilted skywards. It went more slowly than I thought it would and altogether I must have gone outside to check on it five or six times. The last time, when the eclipse was nearly total, I saw that the clouds were about to finally put an end to the performance. They'd cooperated for a while, but would no longer.

This was when my sister finally arrived, forty-five minutes late.

I was on the other side of the road when she arrived. I'd gone across to get a better view of the eclipse and saw her. She was carrying two large shopping bags, which were probably as much explanation as there'd be for why she was late.

Instead of crossing back to join her I stood and watched as she pushed through the door into the café. I realised then that I had no interest in seeing her, let alone hearing what she wanted to get off her chest. I was tired of it. It's surprising how hard it can be to forgive a little girl even after all those years.

I looked up and saw the clouds closing in on the remaining sliver of moon, then lowered my gaze to look through the window across the street, where I saw my sister settle herself at the table next to the one I'd been at. Who was she? I wondered. My sister, of course, but beyond that what was there to set her apart from the crowds of others? Our history. Summer vacations. The birthday party when she turned nine and fell down the stairs and we spent the rest of the day at the hospital while she got her cast. The time she came home drunk from a party when she was thirteen. The housewarming present she gave me when I first moved out: a pillow case with Mole and Rat on it, from *Wind in the Willows*, with no idea who they were. A love of gritty cop shows. An aversion to the colour brown. An inability to apologise unless she thought it might get her somewhere.

From my pocket I heard my phone, a text. Through the window across the street I saw my sister put her phone on the table. I didn't bother to see what she'd messaged me. I looked from her to the sky and back again. Then my phone was ringing. My hand automatically went for it, but I stopped. I didn't want to answer. I'd go across the street in a minute. I knew

I would. I'd go in there and sit across from her, and I'd tell her I had been just outside watching the eclipse and she'd say, 'Eclipse? I didn't know there was an eclipse.' And then I'd hear all about how unhappy she was, how she needed things to change, but what she wouldn't talk about was how and why she was unwilling to do anything about it. That part of herself never looked across the table at me.

And that's more or less how it turned out when I did finally wander across. More grumbling, a few tears, and not a word about the ancients and their blind speculation of why the moon went dark from time to time. If I ever thought that what we were going to talk about had a chance of taking that kind of turn, even if it was about something I was ages past wondering about myself, it'd be different. I'd go willingly. I'd come running.

In the end she pulled something from one of her bags. It was a sweater. She'd bought it for the husband she was apparently incapable of leaving, but didn't think he'd like it after all. Did I want it?

I took it. I'd never wear it, but it was an easy way to show my otherwise impossible love for her.

RESET:
IN THE KITCHEN SOMETIME AFTER MIDNIGHT BUT WELL BEFORE DAWN
BARBARA TURNEY WIELAND

stretched thin and limp across the linoleum
the moon throbs in time
to my beaten
heart
sorry to shed its light
on hollowed out and empty chimes
on sobs leached black and white
dragged ankle deep
loud as cloud
hung as helpless
as colourless as
clocks as
soggy curtains set
to muted tone
skinned and boned
tea's gone cold
I forget what time it was
I forgot the time
for runny yolks
so
scrambled
it is

WINTER WASP — LAURA MCKEE

other days he is happy inside other holes
the lure of pockmarked bricks
into the split parts of frames and felled trees

dozy with winter
he has chosen to be in the warm
inside of me somehow

zipped tight in the awkward curl of my ear
he brings all of the secrets
he has overheard from the bees

with a low buzz moan
he pushes further in because
he wants me to hear how he suffers

envy of these things:
their sense of purpose
dance moves

he bends over backwards to listen in on them
to know why they chose hexagons over squares
why honey is theirs

THE TRIBES OF GRASS — NANCY HOLMES

Give me your spikelets, your glumes,
your lemmas and paleas.
Give me your sedges and fescues,
oats and timothies.
Such awns, such ascending,
barbed, beaked, bearded
heart-shaped, bladed.
With collars and bristles,
some crowned, some webbed, some keeled.
Songs succulent, tawny, and sheathed.
Seeds canoed, seeds like pears.
Dances incurved, dances long, swaying, and pale.
Those palatable. Those silky.
The humble and the nodding.
Those that enter the mouths of the grazers.
Marshes, prairies, hillsides, alpine, woods,
pastures, meadows, backyards, parks, fields,
gardens, wastelands, gravel pits, wrecks, deserts, sand:
all yours.
All subject to your spears and your invaders,
your strings and your orchestras.
Where do you not scatter your gestures
and fling your grainy notes?
No savannah exists without you,
no loaf of bread.
You are the feathers of the earth,
that bird of the sun.

THE SECRET NAMES OF OBJECTS
JONATHAN GREENHAUSE

What if every object had a name?   A sock called Steve
or Eugene or Genevieve?
                              Each jacket-sleeve Celine;
Each run in the stocking   a Gulshan or Maybelline.

Each T-shirt armpit hole Laurent;   Each stain a Kristine;
Each forgotten moment
                              a random Antonio or Eve.
There could be names   for where air's no longer there

or for meatloaf sandwiches   & their Daniel wreathes
of festive toothpicks,
                              their 2 slices of bread
& pickles baptised Ludvig,   names to ameliorate

the intolerable loneliness   of not being Ted or Rick.
A secret history of objects
                              so step-stools could be Jude;
a breath for inorganic life,   for neglected multitudes

floundering in anonymity   but rechristened Yuzuki;
an intimate link to launch
                              paper & ink into posterity,
a poem named Mohammed   or Luca   or Beckett.

THE CRANNÓG QUESTIONNAIRE   ALAN MCMONAGLE

How would you introduce yourself as a writer to those who may not know you.
My name is Alan McMonagle and I write short stories, radio dramas and (more recently) novels that may best be described as comedies of desperation.

When did you start writing?
From early childhood I remember hearing a lunchtime radio drama called *Harbour Hotel*. There was a nosey fuss bucket of a woman (I forget her name) who wanted to be in everyone's business. I decided to churn out my own version of *Harbour Hotel* and in the opening scene I produced the dead body of this woman. This outrageous happening allowed me introduce my very own Hercule Poirot style sleuth who (from memory) went by the auspicious name of Hercules.

Do you have a writing routine?
They say Dostoevsky wrote at night and Tolstoy wrote during the day. I have been both.

When you write, do you picture somehow a potential audience or do you just write?
Just write – the responsibility is to the work.

Some writers describe themselves as planners, while others plunge right in to the writing. Would you consider yourself a planner or a plunger?
A plunger.

How important are names to you in your books? Do you choose the names based on liking the way they sound or for the meaning? Do you have any name-choosing resources you recommend?
Very important, and I choose both for the sound and meaning. At the moment I use Twitter, old movie cast listings and Rahoon Cemetery in

Galway.

Is there a certain type of scene that's harder for you to write than others? Love? Action? Erotic?
Every scene I write is difficult.

Tell us a bit about your non-literary work experience please.
I have worked as an office slave, a greeting card seller, and a travel writer. I remember an editor of a travel magazine saying to me, 'Alan, this is supposed to be a paragliding article, not *War and Peace*.'

What do you like to read in your free time?
Novels, short stories, poetry, plays. The whole bit. I also listen to radio drama.

What one book do you wish you had written?
Pedro Páramo, a fragile, enchanting miracle of a book and only novel by the Mexican author Juan Rulfo. Also Flann O'Brien's anarchic *The Third Policeman*.

Do you see writing short stories as practice for writing novels?
The notion that short stories should be regarded as some sort of potty training for the novel is ludicrous. They are separate and equally valid forms. They pose their own and singular challenges.

Do you think writers have a social role to play in society or is their role solely artistic?
You are going to invest yourself in what is of interest to you and what is preoccupying you. In my case this has been character, voice, tone, place. So much of writing is bearing witness. So to some extent it is inevitable artistic sensibility and wider social context will touch off each other, however fleetingly. But for me the initial spark or urge to set something down comes from a very intrinsic place, a place that is light years away from the wider world around me.

Tell us something about your latest publication, please.
My latest publication is my first novel, *Ithaca*. Essentially, it is a quest story, and of the measures my young narrator is prepared to take as he begins to realise that who or what it is he is looking for is possibly a lot closer to home than he initially believes.

Can writing be taught?
I think close reading can be taught. Plus, from a good writing course, I think one can acquire useful habits such as focus and discipline and concentration.

Have you given or attended creative writing workshops? And if you have, share your experiences a bit please.
Eleven years ago I did the MA in Writing at NUI Galway. It allows you sample modules in every writing genre from poetry to hard news journalism – perfect if you are uncertain (as I was) as to what form you want to devote yourself to.
I have also given workshops to beginner writers at the Writers' Centre in Dublin and at various venues nationwide. Recently, I visited a school near my home town. I gave this writing prompt to a class of twelve year olds: *I saw Chopper Fallon walking up the Battery Road carrying an axe.* Straightaway the very first boy in the very first row added this seven-word sentence: *There are no trees where we live.* Genius.

Flash fiction – how driven is the popularity of this form by social media like Twitter and its word limits? Do you see Twitter as somehow leading to shorter fiction?
It was popular before Twitter, surely.
No, I don't. An effective story is as long or as short as it needs to be.

Finally, what question do you wish that someone would ask about your writing, and how would you answer it?
In the run-up to publication of my novel I was asked a question on a radio show that more or less drew a complete blank from me: *What is Ithaca?* Almost one year on and I am in possession of a very snazzy answer to this

question (at least I think I am), and no one is bothered asking me! My snazzy answer paraphrases a quote from the French painter George Braque who was offering an interpretation of his own art: Ithaca is a wound turned towards light.

Finally, finally, some Quick Pick Questions:

E-books or print?
Print.
Dog or cat?
Dog.
Reviews – read or don't read?
Read.
Best city to inspire a writer: London, Dublin, New York (Other)?
Buenos Aires.
Favourite meal out: breakfast, lunch, dinner?
Dinner.
Weekly series or box sets?
Box sets.
Favourite colour?
Red.
Rolling Stones or Beatles?
Beatles.
Night or day?
Night.

Artist's Statement

Cover image: *Flight 126 (Stars)* by Ruth McHugh

Galway-born artist Ruth McHugh has developed her oeuvre from painting, through sculptural installation into a cross-disciplinary practice.
Underpinning her use of various media has been the development of a socio-cultural research process that engages with the fabric of contemporary existence. The relationship between time, memory, sense of place, identity and architecture features significantly within her works.
Flight 126 (Stars) is a photographic record of an ephemeral sighting on a flight from Italy to Dublin. This illusory image, an instance created by a technical flaw, has the semblance of a cipher or a celestial map.

Biographical Details

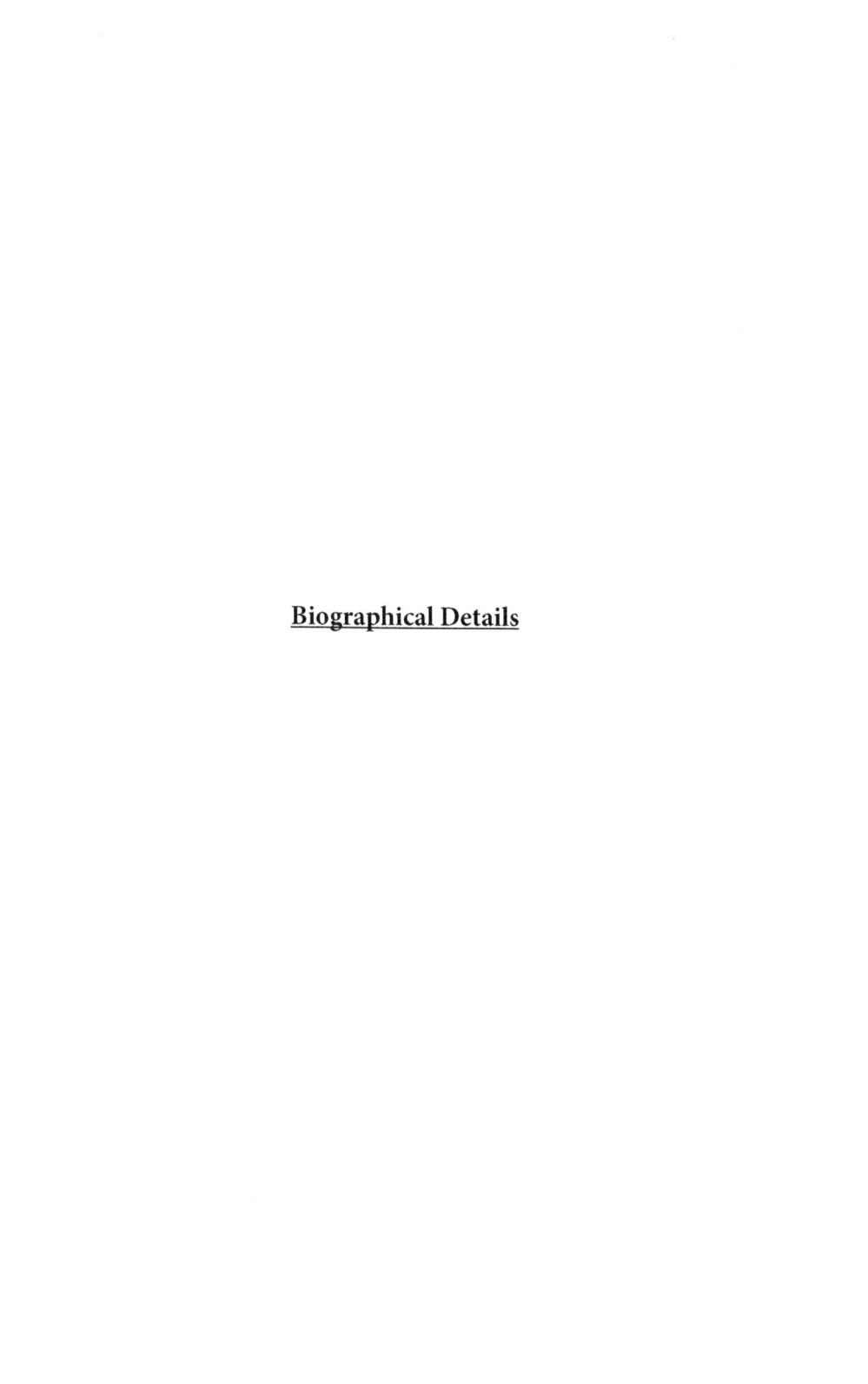

James C. Bassett's fiction has appeared in such markets as *Amazing Stories* and the World Fantasy Award-winning anthology *Leviathan 3*. He is also an award-winning stone and wood sculptor and painter. www.jamescbassett.com.

Byron Beynon's work has appeared in several publications including *Crannóg, Cyphers, The Stony Thursday Book, London Magazine, Poetry Wales, The Yellow Nib* and the human rights anthology *In Protest* (University of London and Keats House Poets). He co-ordinated the Wales section of the anthology *Fifty Strong* (Heinemann). His collections include *Cuffs* (Rack Press), *Human Shores* (Lapwing Publications) and *The Echoing Coastline* (Agenda Editions).

Sasha Burshteyn was born in Russia, and grew up shuttling between Eastern Ukraine and New York City. She graduated from Amherst College with a B.A. in English in 2016 and spent the past year living in five different countries, writing about their experiences with frame-shifting socio-political transitions. She lives, works, and writes in New York.

Lauren Camp is the author of three books, including *One Hundred Hungers* (Tupelo Press, 2016), which won the Dorset Prize. Her poems have appeared in *Asymptote, New England Review, Slice, Boston Review, World Literature Today, Beloit Poetry Journal* and the Academy of American Poets' *Poem-a-Day*. Other literary honours include the Margaret Randall Poetry Prize, the Anna Davidson Rosenberg Award, and a Black Earth Institute Fellowship. www.laurencamp.com

Michael Casey has published four books and numerous poems and short stories, many of them award-winning. Six of his plays have been performed on stage, one in the Henrik Ibsen Museum, Oslo.

Joe Davies' short fiction has appeared in *The Missouri Review, PRISM International, Stand Magazine, Queen's Quarterly, Exile, Grain Magazine, Planet: The Welsh Internationalist, The New Quarterly, The Manchester Review* and previously in *Crannóg*. He lives in Peterborough, Ontario, Canada.

Ellen Denton is a freelance writer living in the Rocky Mountains of the USA. Her writing has been published in over a hundred magazines and anthologies.

Laura Foley is the author of six poetry collections, including, most recently, *WTF* and *Night Ringing*. Her poem *Gratitude List* won the Common Good Books poetry contest and was read by Garrison Keillor on *The Writer's Almanac*. Her poem *Nine Ways of Looking at Light* won the Joe Gouveia Outermost Poetry Contest, judged by Marge Piercy. She has an M.A. and an M. Phil. in English Lit. from Columbia University. She lives in Vermont.

Shauna Gilligan's debut novel *Happiness Comes from Nowhere* was hailed by the *Sunday Independent* as 'thoroughly enjoyable and refreshingly challenging'. She is currently working on an historical fiction novel. She lives in Kildare, Ireland. www.shaunaswriting.com

Jonathan Greenhause's poems have appeared or are forthcoming in *The Dark Horse, The Moth, The Rialto, Southword Journal, The Stinging Fly,* and *Subtropics,* among others. He won the 2017 Ledbury Poetry Competition and the 2017 *Prism Review* Poetry Contest.

Richard W. Halperin's most recent collection for Salmon is *Catch Me While You Have the Light*. His most recent chapbooks for Lapwing are *The House with the Stone Lions* and *Prisms*.

Kevin Higgins is co-organiser of Over The Edge literary events. He is poetry critic of *The Galway Advertiser*. His poetry is discussed in *The Cambridge Introduction to Modern Irish Poetry* and features in the anthology *Identity Parade – New British and Irish Poets* (Ed. Roddy Lumsden, Bloodaxe, 2010) and in *The Hundred Years' War: modern war poems* (Ed. Neil Astley, Bloodaxe, April 2014). In 2014 his poetry was the subject of a paper *The Case of Kevin Higgins, or, The Present State of Irish Poetic Satire* presented by David Wheatley at a Symposium on Satire at the University of Aberdeen. *The Selected Satires of Kevin Higgins* was published by NuaScéalta in 2016. A pamphlet of his political poems *The Minister For Poetry Has Decreed* was published by the Culture Matters imprint of the UK-based Manifesto Press. His poems have been quoted in *The Daily Telegraph*, *The Times* (UK), *The Independent*, and *The Daily Mirror*. His latest collection is *Song of Songs 2.0: New & Selected Poems*, published by Salmon.

Nancy Holmes has published five collections of poetry, most recently *The Flicker Tree: Okanagan Poems* (Ronsdale, 2012). She edited *Open Wide a Wilderness: Canadian Nature Poems* (Wilfrid Laurier University Press, 2009) and teaches Creative Writing at the University of British Columbia Okanagan.

Michael Derrick Hudson's poems have appeared in *Poetry*, *Columbia*, *Georgia Review*, *Gulf Coast*, *Iowa Review*, *Shenandoah* and other journals. He was co-winner of the 2014 Manchester Poetry Prize and was second in the Munster Literature Centre 2016 Gregory O'Donoghue International Poetry Competition. The Poetry Society's National Poetry Competition (UK) longlisted his poem *The Phantom of the Opera Quits Online Dating* in 2017.

Maria Isakova Bennett works for charities, collaborates on projects in galleries on Merseyside, and has just launched a stitched poetry journal, *Coast to Coast to Coast*, co-edited with poet Michael Brown. She was awarded first prize in the Ver Open Poetry Award judged by Clare Pollard, and received a Northern Writers' Award in June. Her pamphlet, *all of the spaces*, will be published by Eyewear in November. She lives in Liverpool.

Brian Kirk's poetry has been widely published in journals and anthologies. He has been nominated for the Pushcart Prize and the Forward Prize 2015 (single poem category). He was selected for the Poetry Ireland Introductions Series in 2013 and was commended in the Patrick Kavanagh Award in 2014 and 2015. His first collection *After The Fall* was published by Salmon Poetry in 2017. He blogs at www.briankirkwriter.com.

Laurinda Lind has poems published or forthcoming in *Anima*, *Antithesis Journal*, *Coldnoon*, *Compose*, *Comstock Review*, *The Cortland Review*, *Deep Water Literary Journal*, *Ekphrasis*, *Here Comes Everyone*, *Josephine Quarterly*, *moongarlic*, *Paterson Literary Review*, *Shooter*, *Soliloquies*, *Sonic Boom*, *Two Thirds North*, and *Uneven Floor*. She lives in the USA, in northern New York State.

Claire Loader was born in New Zealand and spent several years in China before moving to Co. Galway, Ireland, where she now lives with her family. She is the creator of www.allthefallingstones.com and is currently writing a memoir.

Clare McCotter's haiku, tanka and haibun have been published in many parts of the world. Her poetry has appeared in *Abridged*, *Boyne Berries*, *Crannóg*, *Cyphers*, *Decanto*, *Envoi*, *The Galway Review*, *The Honest Ulsterman*, *Iota*, *The Linnet's Wings*, *The Moth Magazine*, *A New Ulster*, *Poetry24*, *Revival*, *The SHOp*, *The Stinging Fly*, and *The Stony Thursday Book*. She was one of three writers featured in *Measuring Dedalus* New Writers 1. *Black Horse Running*, her first collection of haiku, tanka and haibun, was published in 2012. She lives in Co. Derry.

Alison McCrossan writes fiction, focusing on voices she feels are less heard. Currently she is studying IT and living in Cork.

Gill McEvoy has published three pamphlets with Happenstance Press, one of which, *The First Telling*, won the Michael Marks award 2015. She has also published two collections with Cinnamon Press.

Eamon Mc Guinness' poetry has recently appeared in *Poetry Ireland Review*, *Boyne Berries*, *Looking at the Stars*, and *Abridged*. One of his poems was featured on the Poetry Jukebox in Belfast. He was shortlisted for the Strokestown International Poetry Prize 2017. He holds an M.A in Creative Writing from UCD. His debut collection is forthcoming from Salmon Poetry.

Laura McKee's poems have appeared in various journals including *Under the Radar*, *The Interpreter's House*, *The Rialto*, and in anthologies including *Mildly Erotic Verse* (Emma Press). One of her poems toured the island on a bus as a winner of the Guernsey International Poetry Competition.

Ray Malone is an artist, writer and translator currently living and working in Berlin, in recent years dedicated to exploring the lyric potential of minimal forms in a series of projects, of which *soundings* is one, written according to certain pre-determined compositional 'rules'. His work has been published in magazines in the US and the UK.

Susan Millar DuMars' fourth book of poetry, *Bone Fire*, was published in April 2016 by Salmon Poetry. She received an Irish Arts Council Bursary for her stories and has published one short-story collection, *Lights In The Distance* (Doire Press, 2010); a second collection is on the way. Susan and her husband, poet Kevin Higgins, have run the successful literary events series Over the Edge in Galway, Ireland since 2003. She edited the 2013 anthology of fiction and poetry, *Over the Edge: The First Ten Years* (Salmon Poetry). Her blog is: http://susanmillardumarsislucky.blogspot.ie/.

Douglas W. Milliken is the author of the novel *To Sleep as Animals* and several chapbooks, most recently *One Thousand Owls Behind Your Chest*. His stories have been honoured by the Maine Literary Awards, the Pushcart Prize, and Glimmer Train, as well as published in dozens of journals, including *Slice*, *The Collagist*, and *Believer*, among others. www.douglaswmilliken.com.

Okwudili Nebeolisa is a Nigerian writer whose work has appeared in *The Threepenny Review*, *Ambit*, *The Cincinnati Review*, *Erbacce*, *Ruminate*, and *Salamander*. He was a finalist for the 2017 Erbacce Prize and won joint second place in the Okot p'Bitek Prize for Poetry in Translation.

Mary O'Brien writes in English and Irish and has had work published in many poetry journals. She was recently shortlisted for the Francis MacManus short story award and was the winner of Duais Fhoras na Gaeilge 2017 at Listowel Writers' Week. She has published five collections of poetry and is presently supported by Artlinks, Co. Wexford to develop her work in the Irish language.

Ciarán O'Rourke is a winner of the Cúirt New Writing Prize and the Fish Poetry Prize. His poetry has been widely published. His first collection is forthcoming from Irish Pages Press.

Aoife Reilly has been published in *The Lake*, *Message in a Bottle*, *Crannóg 38*, *Boyne Berries*, *Skylight 47*, *ROPES*, *The Ogham Stone*, *The Galway Review*, *A New Ulster*, *Spontaneity.org* and *Tales from the Forest*. Her first collection is *Lilac and Gooseberries* (Lapwing Publications).

Stephanie Roberts has worked featured and forthcoming in numerous periodicals, in Europe and North America, including *Arcturus*, *Banshee*, *The Stockholm Review of Literature*, *Burning House Press*, *Shooter Literary Magazine*, *OCCULUM*, and *The Maine Review*. A finalist in the Eyewear Publishing LTD 7th Fortnight poetry Prize, and the Anomalous Press Open Reading Period. She was born in Central America, grew up in Brooklyn, NY, and now lives just outside Montréal.

Vinny Steed's poems have appeared in the *Galway Review*, *Headstuff*, *Skylight 47*, *Crannóg*, *Into the Void*, *Tales from the Forest*, *The Ofi Press Magazine*, *ROPES*, *All the Sins*, *Boyne Berries*, *Poems in Profile* and in the 25th anniversary edition of *Windows Anthology* and in a Cinnamon Press anthology, *In the Cinnamon Corners*. He won second place in the Westport Arts Festival poetry competition. He has been nominated for The Pushcart Prize.

Lisa C. Taylor is the author of four collections of poetry and one collection of short fiction, *Growing a New Tail*, published by Arlen House in 2015. A new collection of short fiction is due out with Arlen House in the summer of 2018. Her honours include the Hugo House New Works Award for Short Fiction, Pushcart nominations in both fiction and poetry, and along with Geraldine Mills, the Elizabeth Shanley Gerson Lecture of Irish Literature at University of Connecticut. Her fiction and poetry have been taught at University of Connecticut, Norwalk Community College, and Manchester Community College. She has recent or forthcoming work in *Tahoma Literary Review*, *WomenArts Quarterly Journal*, *Map Literary*, and *Gravel*. She teaches creative writing at Eastern Connecticut State University and Nichols College and conducts workshops and master classes for writers in the US and Ireland.

Ruth Thompson is the author of three books of poetry: *Crazing*, *Woman With Crows*, and *Here Along Cazenovia Creek*. Her poems have won New Millennium Writings, Chautauqua, and Tupelo Quarterly awards, have been nominated for the Pushcart Prize and have been choreographed and performed by Shizuno Nasu. Current work appears or is forthcoming in *Poetry Flash*, *bosque*, *American Poetry Journal*, *Tar River Poetry Review*, and *New Millennium Writings*. She teaches writing and operates a small literary press in Hilo, Hawai'i. www.ruththompson.net.

Jean Tuomey has been published in *Crannóg*, *Fish Anthology*, *Stony Thursday* and *Washing Windows?* She facilitates writing groups in Mayo and trained as a writing facilitator with the National Association for Poetry Therapy in the US. She currently lives in Castlebar, Co. Mayo.

Barbara Turney Wieland is a visual artist and a poet who also dabbles in short story. Her poems have been published in such outlets as *Narrow Road*, *Poetry Quarterly* and *Jazz Cigarette*. She is a member of the Geneva Writers' Group.

Karla Van Vliet is the author of two collections of poems, *From the Book of Remembrance* and *The River From My Mouth*. She is an Edna St. Vincent Millay Poetry Prize 2016 finalist and was nominated for a 2015 Pushcart Prize and for a 2016 Best of the Net. Her poems have appeared in *Poet Lore*, *Blue Heron Review*, *The Tishman Review*, *Green Mountains Review*, *Crannóg* and others. Her chapbook *Fragments: From the Lost Book of the Bird Spirit* is forthcoming from Folded Word. She is a co-founder and editor of *deLuge Journal*, a literary and arts journal, as well as the administrator of the New England Young Writers' Conference at Bread Loaf, Middlebury College.

John Wall Barger's third book of poems, *The Book of Festus* (Palimpsest Press), was a finalist for the 2016 JM Abraham Poetry Award. His work appears in *The Stinging Fly*, *The Cincinnati Review*, *Pleiades*, *Hotel Amerika*, and *Best of the Best Canadian Poetry*. He was co-winner of the *Malahat Review*'s 2017 Long Poem Prize. He is on the editing board at *Painted Bride Quarterly*.

Anne Walsh Donnelly's work has been published in various print and online magazines such as *Crannóg*, *The Blue Nib*, *Star82 Review* and *Cold Coffee Stand*. Her stories have been broadcast on RTÉ Radio One. Her poems were highly commended in the Over The Edge New Writer of the Year Award (2017) and commended in the Westport Arts Festival poetry competition (2017).

Maureen Weldon won 'Poem of the Month', Second Light Live, June 2017, for her poem *Midnight Robin*, first published in *Crannóg* 18. She has published five chapbooks, the most recent being *Midnight Robin* published by Poetry Space Ltd, 2014. Her recent publications include *Indra's Net International Poetry Anthology* in aid of The Book Bus charity. *Open Mouse* ezine, *Ink Sweat & Tears*, *Poetry Scotland – Keep Poems Alive International*. Eight of her poems have been translated into Ukrainian and published in Vsesvit, 2017.

Kory Wells lives in Murfreesboro, Tennessee, where she was selected as the city's inaugural poet laureate in 2017. She is the author of *Heaven Was The Moon* (March Street Press). Her work appears or is forthcoming in *APIARY Magazine*, *James Dickey Review*, *Helen*, and *STIRRING*, among other publications. Read and hear more of her poetry at korywells.com.

Alice West was highly commended in the Foyle's Young Poet of the Year 2015 and the Basil Bunting Award for young poets with poems published in each of their anthologies and online. Her work is forthcoming in BustaRhyme's 2017 anthology. She is currently a student of psychology.

Stay in touch with

Crannóg

@

www.crannogmagazine.com

Lightning Source UK Ltd.
Milton Keynes UK
UKOW01f1522080218
317552UK00002B/83/P